For Adele and Samuel
~ IG

For Rebecca
~ TW

This edition produced for The Book People Ltd
Hall Wood Avenue, Haydock, St Helens WA11 9UL,
by LITTLE TIGER PRESS
1 The Coda Centre, 189 Munster Road, London SW6 6AW
First published in Great Britain 2001
Text © 2001 Isobel Gamble
Illustrations © 2001 Tim Warnes
Isobel Gamble and Tim Warnes have asserted their rights
to be identified as the author and illustrator of this work
under the Copyright, Designs and Patents Act, 1988.
Printed in China
• ISBN 1 85430 706 1
1 3 5 7 9 10 8 6 4 2

Isobel Gamble and Tim Warnes

Who's That?

TED SMART

Daisy Dog was tired.
She made her way to
her cosy kennel for
an afternoon snooze.
But . . .

"Who's that sleeping
in my kennel?" she
yawned.

Snorter trotted and snorted all the way home, only to discover that someone had got there before him.

"Who's that dozing in my sty?" he oinked.

"It's Dabble Duck!
This is *my* sty, Dabble.
It's for pigs, not ducks."

Feeling very tired, Dabble swam across the pond to her nest. But two long fluffy brown ears were poking up from behind the rushes.

"Who's that snoozing in my nest?" quacked Dabble.

Racer skipped and hopped across the meadow, but he spotted a bushy tail sticking out of his cosy burrow. *Someone* was there already.

"Who's that snoring in my burrow?" he twitched.

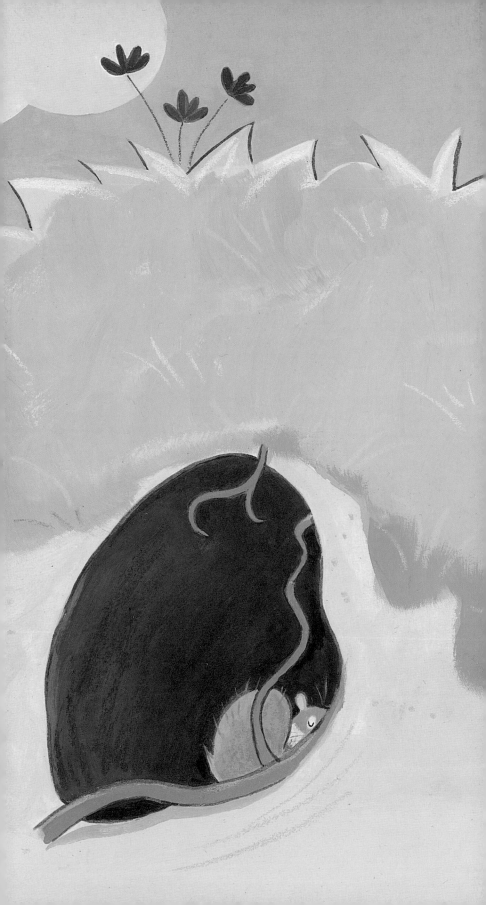

"It's Sandy Squirrel!
This is *my* burrow, Sandy.
It's not big enough for
both of us."

Sandy scrambled off up
a tree, looking forward
to a long deep sleep.
She noticed two tiny
pink ears popping up
between the leaves.

"Who's that snoozing in
my drey?" she sniffed.

"It's Merry Mouse!
This is *my* drey, Merry.
You don't belong here."

Merry scuttled back
to her own little
mousehole, only to
discover someone
very big and *very*
furry lying right
across it.

"I know who th-that
is," she squeaked.

"It's C-Caspar Cat! D-do you think I could get to my m-mousehole?"

It was Merry's lucky day. Caspar was far too tired to catch mice. He slowly got up and made his way to his very own bed. But someone cute and cuddly was already sleeping there.

"Who's that sleeping beneath my favourite blanket?" he miaowed.

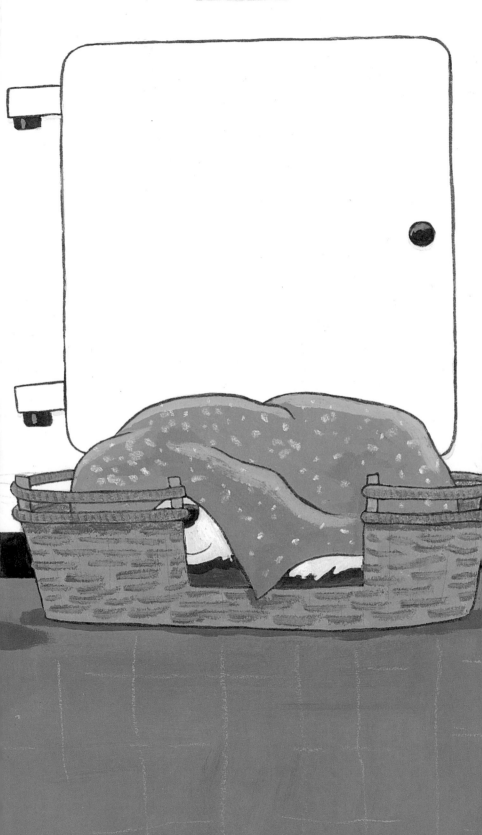

"It's Poppy Puppy!
This is *my* basket.
You should be snuggled
up in your own bed."

Poppy padded wearily home. It was getting late and she was very tired. But . . .

"Who's that cuddled up in my kennel?" she yelped.

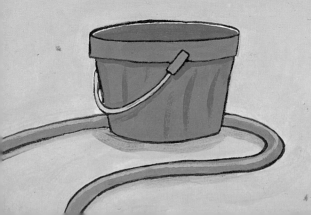

"Hooray!
It's Mummy."

"So *there* you are, Poppy,"
said Daisy Dog thankfully.
"It's long past bedtime.
Now off you go – to sleep."